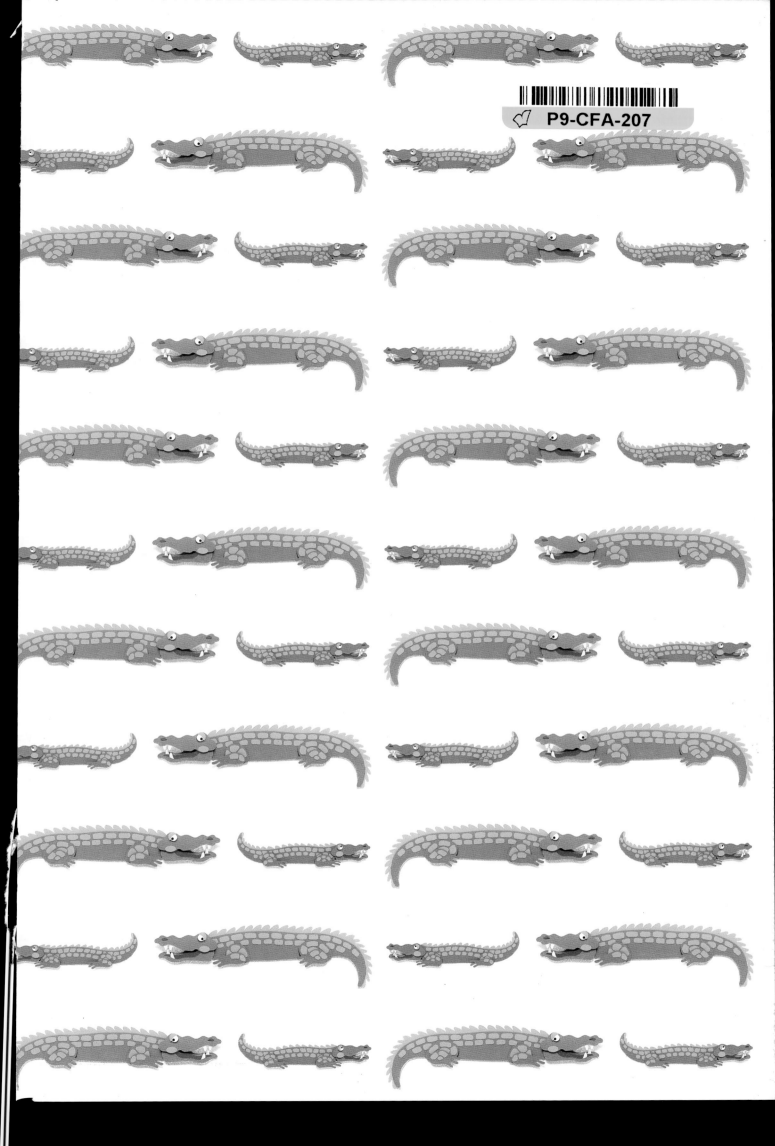

A DORLING KINDERSLEY BOOK

I would like to acknowledge my debt of gratitude to three women:

*To Gerri Hall Gray, a storyteller and children's librarian who long ago
said to me, "Tell the story as though it happened to you yesterday."*

To Julie Bates, a reading teacher who introduced me to stick puppets.

*And to JoAnn Seaver, who invited me to co-teach Children's Literature
in 1979 and from whom I learned much of what I know about using
books with children.*

—Barbara Baumgartner

For my mother, my friend, with love.

—Judith Moffatt

First American Edition, 1994

2 4 6 8 10 9 7 5 3 1

Published in the United States by
Dorling Kindersley Publishing, Inc., 95 Madison Avenue
New York, New York 10016

Library of Congress Cataloging-in-Publication Data
Baumgartner, Barbara.
Crocodile! Crocodile! Stories told around the world / retold by
Barbara Baumgartner: illustrated by Judith Moffatt.
—1st. American ed.
p.   cm.
Contents: Crocodile! crocodile!—Crocodile hunts for the monkey
—The squeaky old bed—How the chipmunk got his stripes
—The grateful snake—Sody saleratus.
ISBN 1-56458-463-1
1. Tales. [1. Folklore.] I. Moffatt, Judith. ill.
II. Title.

PZ8. 1. B345Cr 1994   93-28027
398.24'52—dc20   CIP
[E]   AC

Color reproduction by DOT Gradations Ltd.
Printed in Hong Kong by Imago

CROCODILE!
CROCODILE!

STORIES TOLD AROUND THE WORLD

For Caitlin
♡ Judith Moffatt
1994

RETOLD BY BARBARA BAUMGARTNER

ILLUSTRATED BY JUDITH MOFFATT

DORLING KINDERSLEY
LONDON · NEW YORK · STUTTGART

CONTENTS

CROCODILE! CROCODILE!
A folktale from India

CROCODILE HUNTS FOR THE MONKEY
A folktale from India

THE SQUEAKY OLD BED
A folktale from Puerto Rico

CROCODILE! CROCODILE!

A folktale from India

A monkey was swinging from branch to branch, high in his tree. Sometimes he would stop to eat a piece of fruit. He could see crocodiles swimming in the river below, so he made up a song about them:

"Crocodile! Crocodile!
You have such big teeth!
Crocodile! Crocodile!
Please don't chase me!
Crocodile! Crocodile!
Will you be my friend?"

Now one day a hungry young crocodile boasted to the wise old crocodile, "I am going to catch one of those monkeys and eat him."

"You will never be able to do that," said the wise old crocodile.

"Don't you know that crocodiles do not travel on land and monkeys do not swim in the water? Besides, monkeys are more cunning and clever than you are."

But the crocodile began to think and plan how to catch a monkey. Finally he had an idea. He called one of the monkeys. "Hello, Monkey. How would you like to go to the island where the fruit trees grow?"

"I would like that," said the monkey. "But there is water all around the island, and I can't swim."

"How would you like to ride there on my back?" asked the crocodile.

"That is very kind of you," said the monkey, and he swung down from his tree and climbed onto the crocodile's back.

The crocodile began swimming
out into the river.

"What a nice ride!" said the monkey.

"Let's see how you like **this**!" said the crocodile.

Then the crocodile dived deeply down into the
river. The poor monkey held on tightly. He was so
scared he would drown!

When the crocodile came back up out of
the water, the monkey was coughing and
choking. "Oh, Crocodile," he cried,
"how could you do that to me? You
know I can't swim!"

"Ah-ha!" said the crocodile. "First
I am going to drown you and
then I will eat you!"

The little monkey was so scared that his heart was going pit-pat, pit-pat. He thought to himself, *How can I get this crocodile to take me back to land?*

Then the monkey got an idea, and he said, "Oh, you're going to eat me? It's too bad I didn't bring my heart with me."

"Your heart?" asked the crocodile.

"Yes," said the monkey. "My heart is the tastiest part of me. But I left it back in my tree."

The crocodile began to turn around and start back toward the land. "We'll go get your heart now," he said.

The monkey said, "But what about the island with the fruit trees?"

"We'll go there later," said the crocodile. "Now we must go get your heart."

 As soon as the crocodile reached the riverbank, the monkey jumped onto dry land and ran up to the top of his tree.

Then he called out, "Crocodile, my heart is up here. You'll have to come up here to get it."

Then the crocodile saw that the monkey had outwitted him, and he thrashed his tail in anger.

That night the monkey decided to get away from the crocodile, so the monkey moved down the river to another tree. He hoped that he would always be safe from that hungry crocodile.

CROCODILE HUNTS FOR THE MONKEY

A folktale from India

For several days the monkey was not bothered by the hungry crocodile. But one morning the crocodile swam farther down the river than he usually did. He was surprised and pleased when he saw his favorite monkey. He watched as the monkey jumped from the riverbank to a rock and from a rock to the island where the fruit trees grow.

The crocodile thought to himself, *Ah-ha! The monkey will stay on the island all day eating fruit. Then, when evening comes, he will jump onto that rock to get to his home on the riverbank. If I lie on that rock, I can catch the monkey and eat him.*

As the sun was beginning to set, the monkey came down to the edge of the island. But before he jumped on the rock, he thought to himself, *That rock looks higher than usual. I wonder if the crocodile is lying on it. Let's see if I can trick him again.*

Then he called loudly, "Hello, Rock."

Of course, there was no answer.

Again the monkey called, "Hello, Rock."

Again there was no answer. Then the monkey said very loudly, "That's funny. My rock doesn't seem to be talking to me tonight. I hope that nothing is wrong."

When the crocodile heard him say that, he thought to himself, *Why, this rock must talk to the monkey. If he calls again, I'll have to answer.*

Just then the monkey called again, "Hello, Rock."

Crocodile answered, "Hello, Monkey."

The monkey said, "Crocodile, is that you lying on my rock?"

"Yes," said the crocodile, "I am waiting to eat you."

The monkey pretended to be scared. "Oh, dear," he said. "I guess there's no hope for me. You might as well just open your mouth and I'll jump right in."

But the monkey knew that when crocodiles open their mouths wide, their eyes shut tight. So the monkey jumped. But he didn't jump into the crocodile's mouth. He jumped over it and landed on the crocodile's back. Then he quickly jumped to the riverbank and ran up to the top of his tree.

The crocodile looked up at him and said, "Monkey, you are much quicker than I am, and you are more cunning and clever. After this, I will leave you alone."

"Thank you, Crocodile," said the monkey. "But I will always be watching for you anyway."

And that is why crocodiles and monkeys have never been friends.

THE SQUEAKY OLD BED

A folktale from Puerto Rico

Long ago in Puerto Rico, there lived a grandma and a grandpa who were raising their little grandson. Now, the little boy liked to play under the bed. It made a wonderful hiding place, and he could pretend that he was in a secret cave. But when the bed squeaked, the little boy was scared, so he cried, "Boo-hoo!"

Then his grandma said,
"Don't cry, little boy.
That's only the sound
of this squeaky old bed."
One day the grandpa
went to the market
and got a dog for
the little boy.

Every day the dog played under
the bed with the little boy.
But when the bed squeaked,
    the dog barked, "Ruff, ruff!"
    And the little boy cried,
    "Boo-hoo!"
    Then the grandma said,
        "Don't bark, little dog.
        Don't cry, little boy.
        That's only the sound
        of this squeaky old bed."
    One day the grandpa went
to the market and got a cat
for the little boy. Every
day the cat played under
the bed with the dog and
the little boy. But when
the bed squeaked,
    the cat said, "Meow, meow!"
    The dog barked, "Ruff, ruff!"
    And the little boy cried,
    "Boo-hoo!"
    Then the grandma said,
        "Don't meow, little cat.
        Don't bark, little dog.
        Don't cry, little boy.
        That's only the sound
        of this squeaky old bed."

17

One day the grandpa went to the market and got a mouse for the little boy. Every day the mouse played under the bed with the cat, the dog, and the little boy. But when the bed squeaked,

the mouse said,
"Squeak, squeak!"
The cat said, "Meow, meow!"
The dog barked, "Ruff, ruff!"
And the little boy cried,
"Boo-hoo!"
Then the grandma said,
"Don't squeak, little mouse.
Don't meow, little cat.
Don't bark, little dog.
Don't cry, little boy.
That's only the sound
of this squeaky old bed."

One day the grandpa went to the market and got a pig for the little boy. Every day the pig played under the bed with the mouse, the cat, the dog, and the little boy.

But when the bed squeaked,
  the pig said, "Oink, oink!"
The mouse said,
"Squeak, squeak!"
The cat said, "Meow, meow!"
The dog barked, "Ruff, ruff!"
And the little boy cried,
"Boo-hoo!"
Then the grandma said,
  "Don't grunt, little pig.
  Don't squeak, little mouse.
  Don't meow, little cat.
  Don't bark, little dog.
  Don't cry, little boy.
  That's only the sound
  of this squeaky old bed."
One day the grandpa decided
to take a nap on the bed. But when
he lay down, the bed squeaked.
  The grandpa grumbled,
  "Ah, me!"
The pig said, "Oink, oink!"
The mouse said,
"Squeak, squeak!"
The cat said, "Meow, meow!"
The dog said, "Ruff, ruff!"
And the little boy cried,
"Boo-hoo!"

Then the grandma said,
    "Don't grumble, old man.
    Don't grunt, little pig.
    Don't squeak, little mouse.
    Don't meow, little cat.
    Don't bark, little dog.
    Don't cry, little boy.
    That's only the sound
    of this squeaky old bed."
    Just then the bed broke.
The old man fell off.
The little pig ran away.
The little mouse ran away.
The little cat ran away.
The little dog ran away.

    The little boy wasn't hurt,
because the bed didn't fall
on him. And the grandma
just laughed and laughed
and laughed.

HOW THE CHIPMUNK GOT HIS STRIPES

A Native American legend

The Seneca Indians say that long, long ago, the chipmunk did not have stripes. His fur was just plain brown.

One day the big bear, Nyugway* to the Seneca people, was tramping through the forest roaring, "I'm the strongest! I'm the greatest!"

Jehookweiss, the little chipmunk, spoke up: "Who said that? Who said, 'I'm the greatest?'"

Nyugway said, "I said that. I'm the strongest! I'm the greatest!"

Jehookweiss said, "I don't think you're so great."

Then Nyugway boasted, "I'm so great that I can keep the sun from coming up."

"You can't do that," said Jehookweiss. "Nobody can keep the sun from coming up."

"Do you want to bet?" said the bear. "Just to prove how strong I am, I'll meet you here in the middle of the night. Watch and see. I will keep the sun from coming up."

So the two animals met at that place in the middle of the night. Nyugway paced back and forth chanting,

"I'm the strongest!
I'm the greatest!
Sun, don't come up!
Sun, don't come up!"

Every now and then Jehookweiss would say, "You're not the greatest. Nobody can keep the sun from coming up."

Finally the eastern sky began to glow with the light of the sun. Nyugway started shouting, "Sun, don't come up! Sun, don't come up!"

As the sun rose over the horizon, Jehookweiss laughed and laughed. "See! You're not the strongest!"

Nyugway felt so angry that he started chasing Jehookweiss. The little chipmunk ran as fast as he could. Nyugway was getting closer and closer.

Suddenly Jehookweiss came to his hole. But just as he started to run down his hole, the bear's claw scratched down his back, leaving the dark stripes that the chipmunk wears even to this day.

*Nyugway is the phonetic spelling of the Seneca word for "bear." Seneca is not a written language. Nyugway sounds like En-YUG-way. Jehookweiss, which means "chipmunk," sounds like Juh-HOOK-wice.

23

THE GRATEFUL SNAKE

A folktale from China

Long ago in China, there was a mother who was very poor. Her younger son, Zee, was a worry to her. She thought he was very foolish. Often she would come home from working in the rice fields and say, "Zee, did you cook the rice and vegetables for our supper?"

Zee would answer, "Yes, I did. But I saw some hungry children in the street. I gave them the food. I thought they needed it more than we do."

One day she shouted at him, "You foolish boy! We have almost nothing left to eat because you are always giving our food to the poor. Here, take this sack of rice cakes and go! Maybe your brother Chu will hire you to work for him. Do not come home until you can bring something of value."

Zee took the sack of rice cakes and began walking. Soon he came to a river. He sat down on the riverbank, took a rice cake out of his bag, and started to eat it. He noticed a thin snake lying near him on the ground. At first he thought that the snake was dead. When the snake moved a little, the boy fed it a piece of rice cake. When Zee was ready to start walking again, he picked up the snake and put it in his sack.

Zee continued walking for several days, and each time he stopped to eat a rice cake, he gave a piece to the snake. He noticed that each time he took the snake out of the sack, it had grown larger.

Finally Zee said to the snake, "My friend, I have no more rice cakes. I have nothing to feed you. And I cannot go home until I can take my mother something of value."

The snake said, "Put me in the river."
Zee placed the snake in the river.
Like magic, the snake turned into a
beautiful dragon.

The dragon said, "Behind that bush
you will find a horse. Say to it 'Neh, neh,
neh.' You will see what will happen."
Zee thanked the dragon. He walked
behind the bush, took the horse by its
reins and said, "Neh, neh, neh."
Three gold coins fell from the
horse's mouth. Zee put the coins
in his pocket. *This is a wonderful
horse*, he thought to himself.
*I will take it home. Now my mother
and I will have money to buy food.*

After walking one day, Zee came to the house of his brother Chu. He asked if he could stay the night. His brother said to him, "Yes, you can sleep in my house. But you cannot keep that horse in your room. I will put it in the shed."

Zee said, "The horse will give you no trouble at all, as long as you do not say to it, 'Neh, neh, neh.'"

Chu took the horse to the shed, and he said, "Neh, neh, neh." Three gold coins fell from the horse's mouth. He said, "Neh, neh, neh. Neh, neh, neh." More gold coins fell from the horse's mouth.

Chu said happily, "This is a wonderful horse. This is a horse to keep!"

The next morning when Zee was ready to leave, Chu gave him a different horse.

When Zee arrived home he said, "Mother, I have brought home a magic horse. Watch!" Then he said, "Neh, neh, neh." The horse said, "Neigh." But nothing else happened.

His mother said, "You foolish boy. That is just an ordinary horse."

Zee traveled back to the dragon. "My friend," he said, "something is wrong with the horse you gave me. First it gave me gold coins, but now it does nothing but neigh."

The dragon said, "Behind that bush you will find a rooster. Say to it, 'Ko, ko, ko.' You will see what will happen."

Zee thanked the dragon. Behind the bush he found a rooster. He said to the rooster, "Ko, ko, ko." Three silver coins fell from the rooster's mouth. Zee put the coins in his pocket. He thought to himself, *This is a wonderful rooster. I will take it home. Now my mother and I will have money to buy food.*

He picked the rooster up and carried it under his arm. After walking one day, Zee came to Chu's house. He asked if he could stay the night. Chu said, "Yes, you can sleep in my house. But you cannot bring that rooster into the house. I will put it in the shed."

Zee said, "The rooster will give you no trouble at all, as long as you do not say to it, 'Ko, ko, ko.'"

Chu took the rooster to the shed, and he said, "Ko, ko, ko." Three silver coins fell from the rooster's mouth. He said, "Ko, ko, ko. Ko, ko, ko." More silver coins fell from the rooster's mouth.

Chu said, "This is a wonderful rooster! This is a rooster to keep!" The next morning when Zee was ready to leave, Chu gave him a different rooster.

When Zee arrived home he said, "Mother, I have brought home a magic rooster. Watch!" Then he said, "Ko, ko, ko."

The rooster crowed, "Cock-a-doodle-doo!" But nothing else happened.

His mother said, "You foolish boy. That is just an ordinary rooster."

Zee traveled back to the dragon. "My friend," he said, "something is wrong with the rooster you gave me. First it gave me silver coins, but now it does nothing but crow."

The dragon said, "Behind that bush you will find a stick. Say to it, 'Dance, stick, dance' and you will see what will happen. If you want the stick to stop dancing, say 'Teng.'"

Zee went behind the bush and picked up the stick. He said, "Dance, stick, dance."

The stick began to dance around his feet, so that Zee had to jump up and down to keep the stick from hitting his legs. Suddenly he remembered the magic word. He shouted, "Teng!" The stick fell to the ground.

Zee looked at the stick. Then he thought to himself, *I think my brother Chu has been playing some tricks on me. Maybe I can use this stick to play a trick on Chu.*

Zee picked up the stick and started walking toward home. When he came to his brother's house, he asked if he could stay the night.

His brother said, "Yes, you can sleep in my house. But you cannot bring that stick into the house. I will put it in the shed."

Zee said, "This stick will give you no trouble, as long as you do not say to it, 'Dance, stick, dance.'"

Chu took the stick into the shed, and he said, "Dance, stick, dance." The stick began to dance around his feet, so that Chu had to jump up and down to keep the stick from hitting his legs. Soon Chu began to call out, "Help! Help!"

When Zee walked into the shed, Chu said, "Zee, make this stick stop dancing!"

Zee said, "If I make the stick stop dancing, you must give me back my own horse and my own rooster."

"Yes, yes," shouted Chu. "I will give you everything that is yours. Just get this stick to stop dancing!"

Zee shouted, "Teng!" and the stick fell to the ground.

The next morning, Zee started walking home with his own horse, his own rooster, and the magic stick.

When he got home he showed his mother what he had brought. First he said, "Neh, neh, neh." Three gold coins fell from the horse's mouth. Then he said, "Ko, ko, ko." Three silver coins fell from the rooster's mouth.

So Zee and his mother always had money for food. And they lived in peace for the rest of their lives.

SODY SALERATUS
An Appalachian folktale

Once upon a time there lived
a grandma and a grandpa, a girl
and a boy, and their little pet
squirrel. They all lived together
in a cabin in the woods.

One day the grandma went
into the kitchen to bake biscuits.
She took out her mixing bowl.
In it she put flour, butter, and salt.
But when she went to get the
sody saleratus*, she saw
that the box was empty.

The grandma said, "Little boy, little boy!"

The boy ran into the kitchen. "Hi, Granny," he said. "What can I do for you?"

The grandma said, "Go down to the corner store and ask the storekeeper to sell you some sody saleratus."

The boy ran out the door and down the road, singing:

> "Sody, sody,
> Sody saleratus."

He ran over the bridge and into the corner store. "Howdy, Mr. Storekeeper," he said. "My granny needs some sody saleratus."

The storekeeper sold him a box of sody saleratus, and the boy started home.

But when he got to the bridge, a great big bear jumped up and roared, "I'm going to eat you and your sody saleratus." Then he swallowed the boy whole.

Back at the cabin, the grandma and the grandpa, the girl and the pet squirrel all waited for the boy. But he didn't come back.

After a while the grandma said, "Little girl, you go down to the corner store and tell your brother to hurry home."

So the girl skipped out the door and down the road, singing:

"Sody, sody,
Sody saleratus."

She skipped over the bridge and into the corner store. "Howdy, Mr. Storekeeper," she said. "Did my brother come in here?"

"Yes, he did," said the storekeeper. "I sold him some sody saleratus, and he started home. But he might have stopped to play along the way."

"Thank you," said the girl. "I'll go look for him." And she started home.

But when she got to the bridge, the great big bear jumped up and roared, "I ate up a little boy and his box of sody saleratus. And I'm going to eat you, too!" Then he swallowed the girl whole.

Back at the cabin, the grandma, the grandpa, and the pet squirrel all waited, but the girl didn't come back.

The grandma said to the grandpa, "I can't bake biscuits without sody saleratus. You go down to the corner store and tell those children to hurry on home."

So the grandpa walked out the door
and down the road, grumbling:

"Sody, sody,
Sody saleratus."

He walked over the bridge and into the
corner store. "Howdy, Mr. Storekeeper," he
said. "Did you see my boy and girl
come in here?"

"I sure did," said the storekeeper. "I sold
the boy some sody saleratus. Then he
started home. The girl came looking for
him, and she started home, too. They
might have stopped to play by the
side of the road."

The grandpa thanked the
storekeeper, and he started home.

But when he got to the bridge, the
great big bear jumped up and roared,
"I ate up a little boy and his box of
sody saleratus. I ate a little girl.
And I'm going to eat
you, too!" Then he
swallowed the
grandpa whole.

Back at the cabin, the grandma and the pet squirrel waited. And they waited. At last the grandma said, "My goodness, I can't get anything done right around here unless I do it myself!"

The grandma stamped out the door and down the road, grumbling:

"Sody, sody,
   Sody saleratus."

She stamped over the bridge and into the corner store. "Mr. Storekeeper," she said, "did you see my boy come in here?"

"Yes, I did," said the storekeeper. "I sold him some sody saleratus and he started home again. The girl and the grandpa came looking for him. But they started home, too."

The grandma thanked the storekeeper, and she started home.

But when she got to the bridge, the great big bear jumped up and roared, "I ate a little boy and his box of sody saleratus. I ate up a little girl; I ate up an old man. And I'm going to eat you, too!" Then he swallowed the grandma whole.

Back at the cabin, that little squirrel was still waiting. And he was hungry!

He ran out the door and down the road, singing:

"Chip, chip, chip, chip,
Chip, chip, chip, chip,
Chip, chip."

That little squirrel ran over the bridge and into the corner store. He hopped up on the counter and he said, "Chip, chip, chip, chip, chip!"

"My goodness," said the storekeeper. "Don't tell me they **all** stopped to play by the side of the road!"

Then the little squirrel jumped down to the floor. He ran out the door and started home.

But when he got to the bridge, the great big bear jumped up and roared, "I ate up a little boy and his box of sody saleratus.

I ate up a little girl, an old man, and an old woman. And I'm going to eat you, too!"

"Oh, no, you're not," said the little squirrel. Then he ran up the nearest tree, the way squirrels do.

The great big bear said, "If you can do it with your little legs, I can do it with my big ones."

Then that bear started to climb the tree.

Now that squirrel was scared, so he ran out on a branch, the way squirrels do.

The great big bear said, "If you can do it with your little legs, then I can do it with my big ones."

Then that bear started to crawl out on the branch.

The squirrel was
so scared that he
jumped from one
tree to another, the
way squirrels do.

The great big bear said, "If
you can do it with your little legs,
then I can do it with my big ones."

The bear tried to jump toward the second tree.
But he missed, and he fell flat on the ground, and
he split wide open.

Out climbed the grandma, the grandpa, the girl,
and the boy, still carrying the box of sody saleratus.
They all walked home together, singing:

"Sody, sody,
Sody saleratus!"

When they got home, the grandma stirred a teaspoon of the sody saleratus into the mixture of flour, salt, and butter. Then she added a little milk, stirred up those biscuits, rolled them out, and put them on the pan to bake in the oven.

When they were nice and brown, the grandma took the biscuits out of the oven.

The grandma ate one biscuit. The grandpa ate two biscuits. The girl ate three biscuits. And the boy ate four biscuits.

But that squirrel was so hungry that he ate 535 biscuits before he was full!

*Sody saleratus sounds like SO-dee sall-uh-RAY-tus. This is an old-fashioned name for baking powder. Without it, the biscuits would be flat and tough instead of light and fluffy.

BRINGING THE STORIES TO LIFE WITH STICK PUPPETS

I first began using puppets with school-age children because I wanted them to have the opportunity to play with a story by retelling it in their own words. I also discovered that, while I might read the story aloud to introduce it, by the time we had acted it out a couple of times, I knew the story well enough to tell it. So stick puppets have also become a way of learning a story.

As I observe children manipulating puppets, I see that they focus on and speak **through** the puppet. This is less intimidating than being the actor on a stage, where all eyes are on you as you speak.

I encourage children to tell the stories in their own words, and I notice that in retelling the story, the children often add to or expand on the story's meanings.

Acting Out the Stories

After they have read or listened to some of the stories in this book, children may enjoy acting them out. Using stick puppets enables one person to present a puppet play with several characters.

Making the Puppets

The easiest puppets are made by drawing just the head of each character on paper. Some people like to draw stick figures on card. Cut-paper illustrations, such as the ones Judith Moffatt has made here, can be used as an attractive and interesting alternative to drawings. Several colors should be used to make the puppets look more exciting. Tape a popsicle stick or tongue depressor to the back of the card to make a holder.

Presenting the Puppet Play

Each puppet is held by its stick and "walked" around a small table. If the story has a lot of characters, such as "The Squeaky Old Bed," a puppet stage can be made by turning a table on its side. When more than two characters need to appear at once, some of them can be taped to the edge of the table.

Don't try to memorize the stories; they should be told in the puppeteer's own words. For instance, at the beginning of "Crocodile! Crocodile!" the crocodile puppet could say something about how hungry he is. In this way children not only learn the story, but use their imaginations to expand and enrich it.

ABOUT FOLKTALE SOURCES

As a children's librarian and storyteller, I am intrigued by old stories that have been passed down orally—often for hundreds of years before anyone thought to write down the words. No matter how many versions of a folktale you hear or read, you will discover that each storyteller brings his or her own voice and meaning to the tale: this is the element that makes storytelling such a fascinating and rewarding experience for me.

I've listed some other versions of the stories that I've collected in this volume:

- "Crocodile! Crocodile!" and "Crocodile Hunts for the Monkey"—*The Monkey and the Crocodile*, illustrated by Paul Galdone (Seabury Press, 1969).
- "The Squeaky Old Bed"—*The Tiger and the Rabbit and Other Tales*, collected by Pura Belpré (Lippincott, 1965).
- "How the Chipmunk Got His Stripes" —I first heard this story told by Bill Crouse, a member of the Allegheny River Indian Dancers. There is a printed version in *How the People Sang the Mountains Up*, collected by Maria Leach (Viking, 1967).
- "The Grateful Snake"—*Tales from Old China*, retold by Isabelle Chang (Random House, 1969).
- "Sody Saleratus"—*Grandfather Tales*, collected by Richard Chase (Houghton Mifflin, 1948).

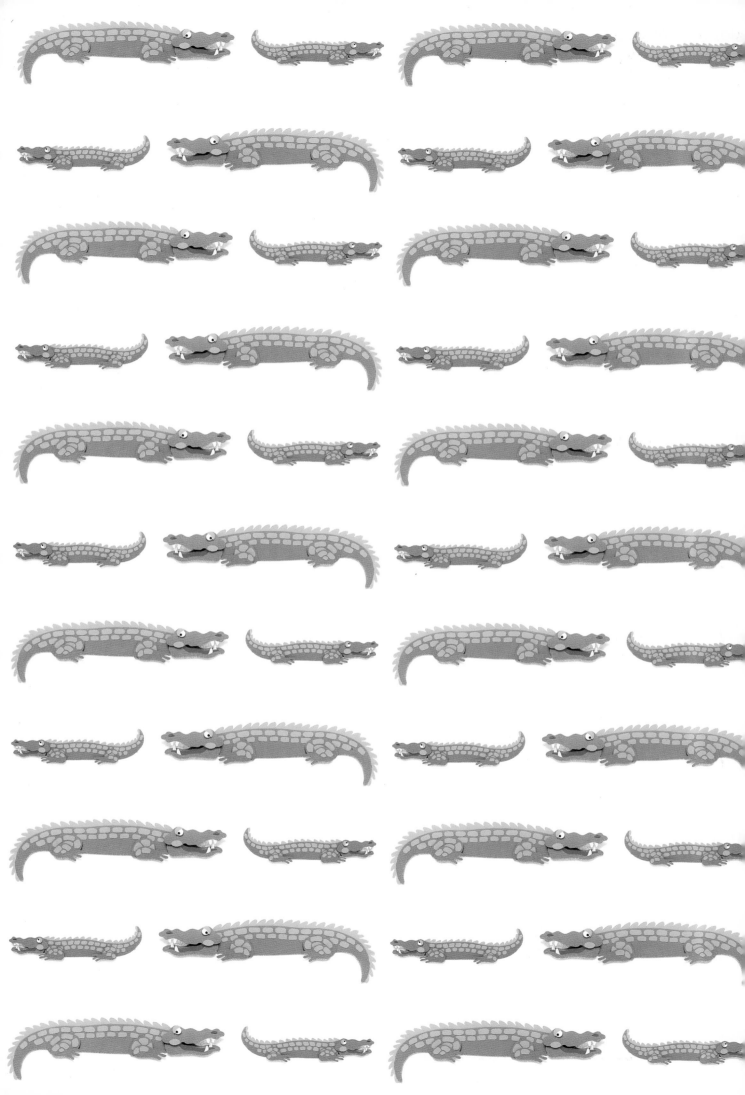